The True Story of
SEA FEATHER

Lois Szymanski

4880 Lower Valley Road, Atglen, Pennsylvania 19310

Other Schiffer Books By The Author:
Grandfather's Secret. ISBN: 978-0-7643-3535-8. $12.99
Out of the Sea, Today's Chincoteague Pony. ISBN:978-0-87033-595-2 $14.95

Designed by "Sue"
Type set in Lydian Csv BT/Zurich BT

ISBN: 978-0-7643-3609-6
Printed in China

Schiffer Books are available at special discounts for bulk purchases for sales promotions
or premiums. Special editions, including personalized covers,
corporate imprints, and excerpts can be created in large quantities for special needs. For
more information contact the publisher:

Published by Schiffer Publishing Ltd.
4880 Lower Valley Road
Atglen, PA 19310
Phone: (610) 593-1777; Fax: (610) 593-2002
E-mail: Info@schifferbooks.com

For the largest selection of fine reference books on this and related subjects,
please visit our web site at **www.schifferbooks.com**
We are always looking for people to write books on new and related subjects.
If you have an idea for a book please contact us at the above address.

This book may be purchased from the publisher.
Include $5.00 for shipping.
Please try your bookstore first.
You may write for a free catalog.

In Europe, Schiffer books are distributed by
Bushwood Books
6 Marksbury Ave.
Kew Gardens
Surrey TW9 4JF England
Phone: 44 (0) 20 8392 8585; Fax: 44 (0) 20 8392 9876
E-mail: info@bushwoodbooks.co.uk
Website: www.bushwoodbooks.co.uk

Chapter One

Shannon squirmed in her seat. Even though they'd left at the crack of dawn, she was pumped with energy. Any other time, the rhythmic rocking of the van would have lulled her to sleep, but she was too excited about the trip. The family traveled to Chincoteague Island in Virginia every year to see the annual Pony Penning. But this year was different. This year she felt on the verge of something big.

Shannon felt the jab of a knee in her ribs as her little sister, Ashley, uncurled her legs.

"Move over," Ashley moaned restlessly. "I'm trying to sleep!"

"How can you?" Shannon grumbled.

"I'm tired."

"But we're going to Chincoteague!" Shannon found it hard to believe that anyone could go to sleep when they were on the way to the islands where wild ponies lived. She couldn't wait to watch them swim the bay from Assateague Island to Chincoteague. And then there would be the auction where the foals would be sold. "We're going to see the ponies," she said. "For Pete's sakes, that's too exciting for sleep!"

Ashley rubbed her eyes irritably. "We've seen them a million times before."

"Not a million."

"Okay, not a million. But we've seen them lots of times."

Mom leveled a look at them from the front seat. "Let's not argue," she suggested. She turned forward again to help Dad watch traffic.

Shannon ran a hand over the blonde bun in her hair and adjusted the pillow behind her back. She wished she could be as calm as her little sister. Had she been that unconcerned two years ago, when she was eight years old? She didn't think so. She couldn't remember a time when she didn't get excited about horses of any size, shape, or color, and there was something special about the wild ponies that lived on Assateague Island. Ever since she had read *Misty of Chincoteague*, and *Stormy, Misty's Foal*, she'd been in love with them.

Adding to Shannon's excitement was a feeling she had deep inside. It was an overwhelming certainty that something good was about to happen. Maybe even great!

She watched her sister stretch out a leg. More of the space on her side of the seat disappeared. She was tempted to crawl into the last seat, even if it was piled high with suitcases and a large beach raft. But Mom would have insisted on a seatbelt and the seatbelts in the back seat were buried.

Shannon pushed a leg against her sister's thigh, grumpily. "You're too calm!" she growled. She touched the wad of green in her pocket. It was thick and full of the promise of things to come. "I'll tell you a secret," she offered.

Ashley opened an eye. There was a flicker of interest. She sat up, pulling the Afghan tightly around her shoulders and waited.

At once Shannon wished she'd kept her mouth shut, something she knew she could not count on her sister to do. But Ashley was staring, eyes round and expectant, so she plunged on. She pushed aside a strand of Ashley's long blonde hair. "I have three-hundred and ninety-eight dollars saved," she whispered into her sister's ear. "That's almost four hundred dollars!"

She said it proudly, for she had worked hard for her aunt and uncle at their carnival company, going to fairs and carnivals all over the county to earn the money. She had spent countless hours picking up darts, sweeping up the tiny burst balloon bits, and making change for folks who paid one dollar to throw three darts. Some of them had walked away with a prize. Others had not. Shannon's prize was in her pocket, a roll of money she had saved for this trip, money that could make her dream come true.

Ashley rubbed her ear ferociously and glared at Shannon. "I've told you a million times not to do that to me," she said angrily. "All you did was tickle my ear and give me chills, and I didn't hear a word you said!"

"Girls!" Mom's stern warning came from the front seat. "Why don't you take a nap? It will be hours until we get to the island."

"I was trying to!" Ashley declared.

Shannon put an arm around her sister firmly. This time she whispered loudly. "Listen up, pip-squeak. I'm only going to say this one more time."

Ashley started to pull away, but a look from Shannon made her sit still.

"I have almost four hundred dollars saved." Shannon spoke slowly and deliberately.

This time Ashley did pull away. "Four hundred dollars?" Her eyes were incredulous. "How did you ever save that much?" Ashley's eyes widened again and she let out a half-squeal.

Mom half-turned to look at them and Shannon could tell that Ashley was fighting to keep her expression calm.

After Mom had resumed her road-watching Ashley finally spoke. "Just think of all the things we can buy on vacation," she spouted. "Cotton candy at the carnival, model horses, salt-water taffy, post-cards... we can even ride all the rides, more than once!"

Shannon shook her head and sighed again. "Let me remind you that this isn't your money."

"It is, if you want me to keep it a secret," Ashley challenged.

"Why you little rat!"

"Well, it's mostly yours," Ashley conceded.

Shannon rolled her eyes in exasperation. If she didn't need her sister on her side she would be tempted to rap her. She tapped Ashley on the top of her head. "Think about it," she prodded. "What do you think we could buy with five hundred dollars?"

Then, a light filled Ashley's eyes.

All right, she thought. Ashley is finally awake!

"A pony!" The words slid from Ashley in a hiss. "Are you going to buy a pony at the Pony Penning auction?

    This time it was Shannon who settled back smugly in her seat. "Every year we ask them, and every year they say we can't afford one," she said softly. "Now I have the money. How can they possibly say no?"

Chapter Two

They were almost to Salisbury before Shannon got up the nerve to ask. Normally, it was an easy question. She asked it each year expecting a no. But this year there was so much on the line. This was the closest she'd ever come to hoping.

Ashley was finally fully awake, propped up on her side of the seat with an electronic game in her hands. Dad had just said something about stopping for food. Mom was in the middle of trying to convince him that he could wait the hour it would take for them to arrive at the campground, when Shannon just blurted it out.

"Can we get a pony this year?"

"No!" Their answers came in unison, like every year before.

"But I have almost four hundred dollars saved."

Silence filled the front seat. Shannon watched Mom and Dad exchange looks, speaking without opening their mouths.

"I didn't know Aunt Kitty was paying you that much?" Dad said.

"I am amazed that you saved all that!" Mom added, "They really did save a lot!" She told Dad. "But, they usually sell for a lot more than five hundred dollars. Last year the average price was nine hundred."

Dad's shoulders relaxed a little and he smiled. "Mom is right. You'd never be able to get one for just four hundred dollars. The ponies cost more now than ever."

"But, Dad." Ashley's voice came in a whine. "Can't we just try?"

There was another moment of silence before Dad spoke again. "Sure," he said. "If you can go from today until the wild pony auction on Thursday without spending your money, and if you really find one for four hundred dollars, we'll allow it. But remember," he added, "The pony you buy will be your responsibility."

"Whoopee!" Shannon squealed.

"You'll have to hold onto your money," Mom reminded them. "Can you go from Monday to Thursday without spending any money?"

"I can," Shannon said.

"Me, too," added Ashley. "I won't spend any of my money either and I'll pitch in to help out.

"How much do you have?" Shannon asked.

Ashley pulled out a tiny black leather purse and snapped it open. "I have all of my birthday money," she said, "and the money Pop Pop and Grammy gave me for vacation, too." She laid the bills on the seat in neat little piles, a twenty, a ten, two fives and three ones.

"Forty-three dollars," Shannon counted.

"That's not all!" Ashley grinned. "Look at this!" She reached under the seat and pulled out a sock. It was knotted at the top and stretched long with the weight of what was inside. She fumbled with the knot, then turned the sock upside down. A pile of coins spilled out onto the seat. A few rolled to the floor.

"Wow!" Shannon said. "Where'd you get all that change?"

"I've been saving it all year," Ashley said. "You'd be surprised at how much gets stuck between the couch cushions, and under the bed."

"That's a lot," Shannon agreed.

"I also got some out of the dryer when I was folding clothes. And some in your top drawer," she admitted sheepishly.

Shannon's eyes clouded over. "You little twerp! I wondered where all my change was going."

"Well, you can thank me for saving it," Ashley said sweetly. "Or else you probably would have spent it on sodas and candy and dumb stuff."

Shannon's anger softened. "I guess you're right," she admitted, "as long as it all goes toward our pony."

"It will."

"Let's count it and see how much we have." Shannon looked from the pile of money to Ashley. She stacked the coins into piles of nickels, dimes, and quarters.

Ashley patted the piles into neater stacks, all except for the pennies, which made a big copper mound on the seat between them. She pulled three pennies out from underneath her. "What color do you like best?" she asked dreamily.

"What do you mean?"

"What color foal is your favorite?"

"Oh." Shannon twisted her bun as she thought. "I don't know. I like them all... but I guess the pintos and the bays the best." She closed her eyes for a moment. She could see a tall bay colt running on the shoreline. The colt splashed through the surf, his long white-stocking legs sending up spray. His brown body was dark with water. His black mane and tail flowed in the breeze.

"Seven dollars and twenty-two cents."

Shannon opened her eyes and the bay foal disappeared. "What?'

"We have seven dollars and twenty-two cents in change. How much does that make all together?" Ashley asked.

Shannon added the numbers in her head. "You have forty-three dollars in bills, and seven dollars and twenty-two cents in change. That makes fifty dollars and twenty-two cents. With my three hundred and ninety-eight dollars, we have four hundred-forty-eight dollars and twenty-two cents!"

"I'll also get a hundred dollars for singing at the Misty Museum," Ashley said. She'd been singing in shows for several years and was excited about singing on Chincoteague. "That makes $548.22. Will that be enough?"

"I don't know." Shannon answered honestly. Then she saw the worry etching her sister's face. The warm feeling of good things to come washed over her again. She put her arms around Ashley and patted her sister's shoulder awkwardly. "Sure, it will be enough," she said as she turned to stare out the window. "It has to be..."

The bay foal materialized again. She could see him running in the reflected glass. His head was held high and his tail made a flag in the wind. Just behind the foal, Shannon imagined a white and brown pinto mare and a trail of wild ponies of every size and color. It just has to be enough, she thought. It just has to be.

Chapter Three

Shannon had three mosquito bites on her legs before the tent was up. She had one on each arm by the time she unrolled her sleeping bag, and another on her neck before Mom finally found the can of mosquito repellent and they all took turns misting their bodies with the pungent spray. Camping at Tom's Cove Campground was always fun,  but at this time of the year there were swarms of mosquitoes.

Soon the tent was up, the gear was unpacked and the family was ready to eat. All through lunch at Etta's Restaurant, Shannon stared out the big picture window and across the bay to Assateague Island. She could see the red and white lighthouse blinking sleepily against the hazy day, but it was ponies she looked for, the ponies that ran wild in her mind. If only they would materialize on the shoreline.

Ashley prodded Shannon with an elbow. "What are you staring at?"

Shannon brought herself out of her daydream and back to the restaurant. "I was looking for the ponies."

"You won't see any," Mom said. "By now the firemen have rounded them up and penned them on the far side of the island to get ready for the swim on Wednesday."

Ashley tapped her fork on the edge of the table. "Can we go see them?" she asked.

Dad's hand settled on top of Ashley's and the tapping stopped. "Sure," he said. "Hurry and finish your lunch and we'll do it today."

A half hour later they were on Assateague. Shannon leaned on the fence-rail and stared at the ponies milling around inside the pen on Assateague. Mom, Dad and Ashley were on the other side, looking at old Broken Jaw. He was a stallion with a broken jaw that caused his teeth to jut out at a weird angle. The strange looking mouth always drew attention from the crowd. Shannon had seen old Broken Jaw many times before and she wandered away. She needed time to see the foals and think. Maybe she could pick out just the right one.

There were pintos of every color combination: black and white, brown and white, red and white, palomino and white, buckskin and white. There were solid colored ones too: chestnut, bay, and palomino. There was even one tall black mare with a blacker mane and tail. She reminded Shannon of Keynote, her favorite horse in the Therapeutic Riding Program back home. Shannon and Ashley had been volunteers for the program for almost two years. For Shannon, it wasn't just the horses. Helping a handicapped kid, who was like herself in every way except the handicap, made her feel good inside.

Shannon watched the foals frolicking together. They raced in circles, chasing each other like children playing tag. One big bay colt chewed on the ear of a sleeping mare. The mare tossed her head from side to side and he dashed away, only to return a moment later to chew on the opposite ear. Soon the mare opened an eye, yawned, and stood. It was obvious that her nap was over! As the mare eyed the colt warily, the youngster sidled over to another mare and began to nurse.

Shannon watched the foal. Like all bays, his body was dark brown with legs that became black at the knees, dark ear tips and a black nose, too. His mane and tail were black, short and stubby, but full of curls. His lashes were long and dark. He closed his eyes and suckled from his mother, occasionally kicking a white leg to shoo away a fly. He looked so peaceful.

"Nice, huh?" Shannon jumped at her dad's deep voice. She had not heard him approach.

"Umm-humm." She answered slowly. "They're all so pretty."

"Look, honey..." Dad hesitated, as if he was having trouble with what he was about to say. "I don't want you to get your hopes up," he said. "You'll only get hurt."

Shannon frowned. "What do you mean?"

"I don't think you'll be able to get a foal, even with the four hundred dollars you have saved."

"Four hundred forty-eight dollars and twenty-two cents," Shannon corrected, "plus Ashley's $100 for singing."

"Yes, it seems like a lot of money, but it probably won't be enough."

"But it might. Last year some colts went for less than five hundred."

Dad shrugged and shook his head sadly. "You did a good job saving your money," he said, "but you have to remember that those were yearling colts. They always go for less money. You can't have a yearling," he said firmly. "By the time they are a year old they are just too wild to train. You wouldn't be able to handle it."

Shannon fought back the tears prickling the back of her eyelids. "All right," she agreed. What Dad said about the yearlings made sense. They might be dangerous. But that didn't mean they wouldn't get a foal. Shannon refused to give up her dream. "We still might find one to buy," she insisted. "A young one."

Dad sighed and rubbed his daughter's back gently. "Those foals are just ten, twelve, fourteen weeks old. They are safe," he said. "But, I don't want you to be too disappointed if you have to wait another year."

That night at the firemen's carnival Shannon and Ashley wandered through the midway, munching on candy apples. Ashley plucked a grey feather from the ground and stuck it in her hair. Shannon smiled. Her sister had collected feathers for years. Already she had a plastic bag at the camp site with two feathers inside.

All at once Ashley took off at a run. "Look!" she yelled. "The raffle pony!"

The raffle pony! Shannon had forgotten about the foal the Ladies Auxiliary raffled off each year!

The raffle pony's pen was surrounded by people. Shannon slid between them to stand next to Ashley. A white nose and two dark eyes peeked up at them. The foal was a filly, a girl pony, with white socks and light brown patches on a startling white body.

The filly had obviously been cleaned up, for the wild ponies were usually mottled with dirt and dust. This one was already used to people and to being touched. She shoved her nose between the rails to be scratched. Shannon caressed the forehead softly. "She's so pretty."

"Should we take a chance on her?" Ashley asked.

"I don't know." Shannon's brow furrowed as she thought. "We should probably save our money.""

"But she's really cute." Ashley ran her fingers through the short, feathery mane.

"She is," Shannon agreed.

The folks standing around the filly began to drift away. The lady in the ticket booth smiled at Shannon. "You never know," she said. "You could be the winner this year."

Mom and Dad came up behind them and Dad chuckled. "These two have saved five hundred dollars," he told the lady. "They think they'll get a foal at the auction. But I'm afraid they're going to be mighty disappointed come Thursday morning."

"Even if you don't buy a ticket," the lady said, "you might want to be here on Friday night when we draw the winner."

Shannon looked at the lady, confused. "Why?"

"Last year the winner couldn't keep the foal, and she sold it to someone in the crowd real cheap," she said with a wink.

Shannon thought that was a good back up plan, just in case they didn't get a foal at the pony penning auction.

The lady's green eyes twinkled. She pushed at a stray lock of yellow hair. "Maybe you should take a chance and buy a ticket on this little filly," she said again. "Just in case... It's only a dollar for five chances."

Shannon rooted in her pocket.

"Do you think we should?" Ashley asked.

Before Shannon could answer, Mom touched her arm. "I'll get you some tickets," she said. She opened her wallet and smiled at the girls. "Five dollars worth," she told the lady.

While Mom and Dad took Ashley to ride the bumper cars and the Scrambler ride, Shannon stood by the foal stroking her soft neck gently. Our odds are getting better, she thought. Kneeling down, she breathed deeply, letting the warm smell of pony wash over her. Somehow, she thought, we'll get a foal. Somehow.

The Ferris wheel left a swirl of colorful lights against a darkened sky as the four left the carnival and headed for the car. Their first day on the island had been full of good things, but it had been a long day.

Only two more days, Shannon thought as they drove to the campground. Then it would be Thursday... the day of the wild pony auction.

Chapter Four

The next day, Mom and Dad took Shannon and Ashley swimming at the beach on Assateague. Shannon stood on the shoreline and the waves lapped over her toes. She smiled as a gull swept low crying Crah, Crah, Crah! It was peaceful here. She loved Assateague. Coming here each year was like coming home. From the wild ponies to the pine trees and myrtle to the salty ocean breezes, everything on Assateague smelled so good. No matter where you drove or 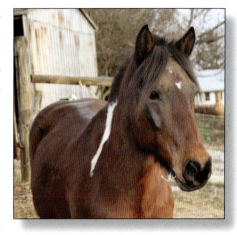 walked or rode a bike, you could find a new kind of wildlife. Egrets and herons strutted through the marshes and canals on high stepping pencil thin legs, searching for food. Then, with the flash of an eye and the stab of a beak, an egret would bring up his fish dinner from beneath the blue-green depths. There were birds of every color, shape, and size. It was no wonder Ashley found so many beautiful feathers on Assateague. There were turtles, too, and Whitetail deer and Sika deer, and even an occasional snake! Shannon didn't like snakes, but she had to admit they never really bothered her. They just slithered away into the brush or water.

Now, Shannon shaded her eyes against the afternoon sun and watched as a school of dolphins came into view. Like a wave, the people on the beach began to stand, first one, then another and another, until everyone was standing, shading their eyes and watching.

"Look, Shannon," Ashley squealed with delight. Shannon looked to where her sister was pointing. A man on a raft was waving to the people on the beach. All at once, he froze in surprise as two playful dolphins circled his raft, leaping into the air and then diving into the ocean before surfacing again.

Shannon watched with Ashley as the dolphins worked their way down the coastline, until they were out of sight.

"Wow!" Ashley sighed. She ran back to her towel and plopped down, but Shannon stood where she was, watching the unfolding power of the ocean. She thought about the dolphins, the warm smells of the island and the animals that lived there. She realized that all of this was what made the Chincoteague ponies special. It wasn't just that they were horses, although that in its self would have been enough. But the Chincoteague ponies were even more. They were the sun, the sand, the untamed beauty of nature... all of it rolled into one. And they were a legend.

Shannon walked to where the family was sitting. Dad was dozing in his beach chair and Mom was reading a book. She smiled when Shannon approached. "Pretty cool, huh?" she asked, and Shannon nodded. The dolphins had been a sight to see.

She settled on a beach towel next to Ashley. "Do you think the ponies really came from a ship wreck?"

Mom looked up from her book, but before she could answer, Ashley did.

"Of course! Where else would they come from?"

Mom closed her book. "Well," she said, "some people believe that colonists who lived on Chincoteague Island in the 1800s put their ponies on Assateague to graze, and to hide them so they wouldn't have to pay taxes on them. Then, when they were ready to take them back, they couldn't recapture them."

"Why would anyone let their horses just run loose?" Ashley asked in disbelief.

"I'm not sure." Mom took a deep breath. "But there is another theory, too. Some historians' think that pirates passing through in the 1700s put a load of stolen ponies on Assateague to graze. They intended to come back and get them, but they never did."

"Pirates!" Ashley's eyes were big. She scooted sand off the towel with her toes. When she plopped her foot back more sand fell onto the towel. She turned to Shannon. "Which story do you believe?"

Shannon looked thoughtful. "I still think the one about the shipwreck is true."

"I can't remember a lot about that one," Ashley said. "Tell it to me again."

Mom pressed her book between her knees and settled deep in the lawn chair. She didn't need encouragement. "Most people believe that a Spanish galleon..."

"A ship," Shannon added.

"Yes, a type of ship called a galleon was carrying ponies from Spain to America to work in the mines. But a storm blew up, tossing the ship like a leaf on the breeze, until it wrecked off the rocks of Assateague. The ponies swam through the mist and rain to the island. All the people onboard were killed, but the ponies survived and their descendants still live on the island today."

When Mom stopped speaking, everyone fell silent. Even Ashley seemed lost in thought. The only sounds were the waves rolling against the shore, the gulls calling overhead, and Dad's soft snores as he dozed in his lawn chair.

Shannon looked out over the ocean again. In her mind, she could hear the call of the shipmaster as he ordered the workmen up on deck. She could hear the frantic screams of the ponies and the crashing of wood as they broke free of their stalls. Then, as the ship went down, she imagined the ponies swimming to shore with their heads raised high in the frothing sea, the rain pounding them as they moved in a line toward land. They probably came ashore exhausted, she thought, picturing a herd of weary ponies, soggy pintos and bays, chestnuts and palominos. Exhausted, she thought, but alive.

Chapter Four

Chapter Five

On Wednesday Shannon awoke to someone shaking her arm. "Come on, Shannon," Ashley said. "We won't get a good spot to see the swim if you don't get up!"

The swim! How could she have overslept? Shannon looked at the little clock that glowed in the dim shadow of the tent. "It's 4:30 in the morning, twerp," she said crossly. "The ponies won't swim until after eight o'clock!"

"Oh, Shannon," Ashley whined. "Get up! I can't sleep, and I don't want to be up by myself."

Shannon moaned and rolled over, placing a pillow over her head. On the other side of the tent Mom and Dad slept quietly, their breaths whooshing in and out softly as they curled in sleep inside their sleeping bags.

"Shannon!"

She felt a pillow thunk her on the head.

"Get up!"

"Oh, you! One of these days I'll get even." Shannon moaned. "Just when you need sleep the most I'm going to wake you up!" She sat up, rubbing sleep from her eyes. "Geez! It isn't even light out!"

"Well, it's almost."

Rolling out of her sleeping bag, Shannon crawled from the tent. The pale rays of first morning light stretched out over the campground, casting golden shadows. Many of the tents were dark and still, but several families were up and about, cooking breakfast on Sterno stoves, gathering at picnic tables for cereal, or walking along the shore, looking out across the bay toward Assateague Island.

"Come on," Shannon said. She gave Ashley's hand a tug and pulled her up from the picnic bench. "Now that you've gotten me up let's walk along the shoreline and see if we can spot anyone on Assateague getting ready for the swim."

The girls could see movement through the mist that rose above the water. It was the firemen on horseback, herding a bunch of milling ponies across the grassy flats toward the bay.

By the time the family made their way to Etta'a Restaurant for breakfast, it was 6:30 a.m. During the meal a radio station kept diners and others informed about the status of the swim.

"The ponies are waiting on the water's edge with a small group of firemen on horseback," the announcer said. "They call these guys saltwater cowboys. Once a year they lose their fire helmets and rubber coats and tack up with Stetsons and cowboy boots."

Shannon listened carefully.

The announcer paused. "The mist is slowly burning off in the sun," he said in a dramatic voice. "On last report, we heard that slack tide will be around 7:55. That's when we'll see some real action, when the ponies swim. Stay tuned," he advised. "We'll keep you up to date, broadcasting live from Etta's Restaurant, overlooking the bay and the swim site."

After breakfast Dad drove to Memorial Park. The family wandered through the tall weeds and pine trees and down to the shore to find the best spot for a good view. On the way, Ashley found the blue, black and white striped feather of a blue jay. She stuck it in her button hole.

Already hordes of people had gathered. Some were in the bay up to their knees. Others had climbed trees and were perching on limbs to get a better view. An announcer with a bull horn kept the crowd advised of what was going on.

"Slack tide will be around 7:55," a deep voice boomed.

Shannon knew the ponies would not swim until slack tide, when the water was at its lowest. It had the least movement then, just before it changed direction.

A volunteer wandered among the crowd selling raffle tickets. "Buy a chance on Queen or King Neptune," a young man told the family. "The first foal ashore is dubbed Queen or King Neptune. It will be raffled off at the carnival grounds as soon as the herds are penned."

Dad pulled a wallet from his back pocket. "I'll take two," he said, handing over two one dollar bills.

Shannon grabbed Ashley's hand. "Another chance to win a foal," she said and they both grinned.

A moment later, Shannon waded out into the water. Ashley tagged behind, feeling for shells with her toes, then picking them up and shoving them in her pockets as she moved deeper into the water.

"Do you think they'll be all right?" Ashley asked. The ponies were bunched up on the other side of the bay. Saltwater cowboys on tall horses were all around, keeping the herd together and ready to swim.

"Sure," Shannon said. Seeing the wave of worry that washed over her sister's face, she put a hand on Ashley's shoulder. "They always do fine."

The swim was about a quarter of a mile. The weakest and oldest ponies, the pregnant mares, and the tiniest foals had already been brought over to the carnival grounds by trailer. Only the strongest, healthiest ponies would make the swim. Shannon wasn't worried. The firemen had been rounding the ponies up and swimming them across the bay for over seventy years, and they'd never lost a foal.

"You know we've seen them swimming on their own in the wild on Assateague," she told Ashley. "And remember that time they were way out in the ocean surf?"

Shannon felt Ashley's shoulders relax. "Yeah! I remember that! The park ranger told us they swim out to get away from the mosquitoes!"

"Slack tide!" the announcer boomed, and Shannon jumped. She looked at her watch. It said 7:54 a.m. "The ponies are about to enter the water. The seventieth annual pony swim is on!"

Chapter Five

Shannon turned to look for Mom and Dad. But all she saw was a sea of milling faces, all waiting for the same thing.

Ashley grabbed hold of Shannon's hand. "I can't see," she whined.

"They're in the water now," the announcer droned. "Up to their knees, now to their neck, and now they are swimming. Please stay clear of the yellow ropes," the announcer chided the crowd. "Stay away from the yellow ropes. That is where the ponies will come ashore."

Shannon stood on her tippy-toes but she couldn't see the ponies anymore. There were too many heads, too many people. Tugging on Ashley's hand, she pulled her sister out of the water and back up the sandy beach. She could see Mom and Dad in the grassy area. Mom lifted her hand and waved. Shannon waved back and then tugged Ashley toward a tall pine tree just off the beach. It took only a moment to shove Ashley up the tree. She scrambled up after her, and the two settled on opposite limbs.

At last, they could see, and just in time too, for the ponies were nearing the shoreline. As they swam, the ponies formed a large triangle in the bay that reminded Shannon of a flock of geese in the sky. With only heads and necks above the water, the ponies seemed to slide forward through the quiet waters, making ripples that expanded out and around them.

"Stay clear of the yellow ropes, folks. Please stand back," the announcer reminded the crowd. "Wild ponies can kick and bite. Please leave a clear path!"

The first fireman on horseback came ashore. He wiped a tired hand over his brow and moved back to make room for the herds. His pants legs were wet and soggy and his horse's body was dark with water stains. When his horse shook the water from her coat, he laughed out loud. Children moved forward, trying to touch his horse.

Shannon watched the herds grow closer. Then a palomino pinto mare scrambled ashore, her mane and tail hanging in soggy ropes. She was followed by a solid brown mare, and a tiny black and white foal. The foal was wet and he looked confused, but he lifted his legs high, prancing and sidestepping his way over to his mother, the brown mare. He clamped himself against her side.

"Look," Ashley said softly. "That must be Neptune!"

Chapter Six

   While the ponies rested, Shannon and her family walked to their car. They joined the line of traffic heading to the carnival grounds. Once there, they waited along Main Street for the ponies to be herded past and into the large pens.

   It was like a parade, the throng of people going down the road on foot, in cars and on bikes, with everyone heading toward the carnival grounds to await the arrival of the ponies. There were lemonade stands all along the way, kids selling colored Kool Aid, lemonade and sodas, and signs advertising parking for just $3.

Shannon settled in a lawn chair and waited with the rest of the crowd near the entrance to the Chincoteague Carnival grounds. She heard a cheer from the people edging the street. The ponies are almost here, she thought.

Across the road from her, Shannon saw a woman wearing a straw hat bend over. She picked up a wispy grey feather and stuck it in the side of her hat. Shannon smiled, thinking of Ashley as she watched the woman.

Then she heard the pounding of hooves and the first pony trotted around the corner. Directed by the saltwater cowboys, the ponies turned into a lane that led to the pens behind the carnival grounds. Dust rose in large brown clouds as the ponies left the street.

"Look, Shannon!" Ashley shrieked. "Look at that one... and that one... and that teeny tiny one!" Ashley's finger jabbed the air, pointing to first one pony, then another, her face flushed with excitement.

When the last of the ponies had passed by, the family followed the crowd through the carnival grounds. They walked under the tall, shady pine trees to the pens where the ponies would live until Friday. The day after the auction, the fireman would swim the ponies back to their island home.

A crowd had gathered around the stage area on the carnival lot. A fireman with dark, curly hair used a microphone to entice the crowd to buy tickets. "King Neptune is a flashy one this year," he said. "Don't miss your last chance to get a ticket. This foal could be yours before the sale even begins tomorrow morning!"

Shannon tugged on Dad's arm. "Get another ticket, Dad!"

"No, Shannon. It only takes one ticket to win and I bought two. That's enough."

Shannon's heart pounded as she watched several young islanders walk through the crowd selling tickets. The foal had been a real beauty. If only they could win it! Then they could use the money they had saved to buy a halter, and a lead shank and food and... Her mind raced with the possibilities.

"We'll draw the winning ticket at one o'clock," the man with the microphone said. "You do have to be present to win this one," he warned, "so be back at one o'clock if you have purchased a ticket."

Shannon looked at her watch. It was almost noon. The morning had gone by so quickly.

"I'm hungry," Ashley announced, and Mom nodded in agreement.

"I'm hungry, too," she said, gesturing toward the sandwich line. Lines were forming at all the carnival rides, too.

"I want a crab-cake," Ashley said, rubbing her tummy, "and French fries, and maybe even some cotton candy."

"Whoa, there, you little bottomless pit," Dad joked. "Let's start with a crab-cake and French fries. Save something until later."

Shannon lagged behind as the others headed toward the food lines. Her eyes lingered on the pens. Each stallion watched over his herd, circling again and again. The mares dosed standing up, while foals stretched out on the ground below, sleeping. Shannon looked from foal to foal. She wondered how Ashley could think of food when they were this close to getting a pony.

After they'd gotten their sandwiches Mom, Dad, Ashley and Shannon walked back to look over the ponies. A look at Ashley's lunch had changed Shannon's mind about eating. The crab cake she'd eaten was one of the best she had ever tasted. Shannon edged in among the crowd. On the far side, she slipped into a narrow space. She leaned against the diamond-shaped, wire fence and watched the ponies milling inside.

The ponies eyed the crowd warily. A few came forward. The foals were awake now, and they moved about, many of them prancing against their mommas' sides. Shannon's eyes fell upon the bays. They were her favorites. Dark brown, rich like mahogany wood, they looked velvety soft, warm, and plush. A bay foal wandered over to the fence and shoved a coal black muzzle against the links. Shannon stretched out her hand slowly, and then cautiously rubbed her palm against the nose. The foal jerked back, darting to his mother's side, but not before Shannon had felt the satiny smooth muzzle. Her heart raced with joy.

"There you are!" Dad's voice reached her about the same time his hand touched Shannon's arm. "We wondered where you had gotten off to."

"I had to get closer, "Shannon explained, her eyes glowing in the aftermath of having touched the foal.

"So I figured," Dad answered dryly. Then he lifted his arm and tapped a finger on the face of his watch. "It's almost time for the drawing," he said.

"The drawing! Well, let's go!"

"Your mom and Ashley have already headed up to the stage," he said.

Shannon took off at a trot. "I'll meet you there," she shouted, leaving her dad behind in clouds of carnival dust.

The crowd that waited around the stage had thickened. Shannon found her mom and Ashley standing off to the side.

"Do you think all these people took chances?" Ashley asked. Her voice was small and sad.

"Probably," Shannon answered. "But remember what Dad said, "It only takes one ticket to win!"

Ashley brushed back strands of blonde hair and looked skeptical. Then her face brightened. She pulled a bright white sea gull feather from her pocket. "Maybe this feather will bring us luck." She stuck it in her hair.

"Do you have your tickets ready?" the fireman asked. He was grinning from ear to ear.

The crowd responded with a mumble of "yeah," and "right here," and groans as they rooted in purses and pockets.

"I can't hear you," the fireman egged them.

"Yes!" the people roared. Some held their tickets high.

Shannon looked at the tickets her mom grasped in a tightly clenched hand. She squeezed her eyes shut, crossed her fingers, and dared to wish.

A lady wrapped in a long white apron turned the crank on the barrel-shaped cage full of tickets. Shannon recognized her from the crab-cake stand.

"Here we go!" The fireman reached deep into the barrel, burrowing his arm up to the shoulder. He rooted around. A moment later he pulled a bright white ticket from the barrel. "Number 1757," he said.

Shannon watched Mom as she read first one ticket, then frowned, and read the next.

"It's me! It's me!" The lady next to Shannon shouted, waving her ticket. But then she frowned. "I can't keep him though," she said. "I only bought a ticket as a donation to the fire department."

Before Shannon knew what was happening, Ashley had grabbed the lady's arm. "We'll take it!" she said excitedly. "We'll give you five hundred dollars straight up, for King Neptune!"

The lady looked confused. Then her face brightened, her blue eyes sparkling. "Will your parents really let you buy the foal?"

"Sure," Shannon said, looking through the crowd for Mom or Dad. Unaware of what was going on, they had moved toward the soda line and were talking, heads down.

"We saved five hundred dollars and Mom and Dad said we could buy a Chincoteague foal," Ashley said. "Wait here," she added abruptly. "I'll go get my dad!" She dashed off.

As Ashley sprinted away, the fireman who had been on the stage approached. He took the ticket from her hand. "Did I hear you right, that you can't keep the foal?"

"Yes," the lady said. "I only bought a ticket to help the fire department."

"Well why don't you let us auction the little guy off right here?"

"These girls," the lady motioned toward Shannon, "offered to buy him for five hundred dollars."

"Heck, we could get a lot more for him than that if you let us auction him off now. Everyone here came hoping to take that little guy home."

The lady looked toward Shannon. "Where are your parents?" she asked, confused.

"My sister..."

"If you're going to let me auction him off for you, you better decide quickly," the fireman urged. "We're losing the crowd."

The lady looked at Shannon once again, and Shannon felt her stomach sink. She already knew what was coming. As she turned to go, she heard the auction begin.

Dad and Mom were at her side less than a moment later, with Ashley tugging them along. She'd lost the feather from her hair.

"It's too late," Shannon said, her stomach wrenching with every word. "It's too late."

Ashley's head dropped until her chin was almost touching her chest. She sighed and grabbed Mom's hand. Shannon turned her back to them. Tears were threatening to erupt, so she bit her lip angrily and began walking toward the pony pens. Just as she entered the shade of the pines she heard the dark haired fireman one last time. "Sold!" he said, "For six hundred and seventy-five dollars!"

Chapter Seven

Ashley sang in the museum in the afternoon. They returned to the carnival.

Shannon ached for the foal that could have been hers. To be so close, and yet so far away... it was worse than never having come close at all. She alternated between being angry at the fireman who had stolen her chance at having King Neptune, to being angry at the woman who had allowed her and Ashley to hope, and then had snatched the hope away.

Riding all the carnival rides twice had been therapy enough for Ashley. She was already chattering about the wild pony auction that would be held in the morning. "Don't worry." she said cheerfully, "We'll find just the right foal there, for sure."

But Shannon was not sure of anything anymore. It seemed their luck was running out. Maybe what had happened to King Neptune was a sign of what was to come.

"How about some cotton candy, sourpuss," Dad asked with half a smile. Before she could answer he shoved a sticky pink cone in her hand.

She took the candy. "I'm not a sourpuss!" She pulled a tuft of spongy pink from the top of the cone, and shoved it in her mouth.

"You sure look it," Ashley commented.

At once, the disappointment and bitter feelings Shannon had been holding in burst from her in a torrent. She turned on Ashley. "How would you know what I'm feeling? It doesn't even matter to you that we lost Neptune! Maybe because you didn't work hard all year at dumb old carnivals to save money! You just fell into my plan!"

Ashley's eyes went wide and she took a step back. She opened her mouth to speak, but before she could, Shannon continued. She flung her arms wide, waving the cotton candy. "This is just another one of those dumb old carnivals, and I was dumb to think that it would be any different!"

"I do care, Shannon," Ashley said. Her bottom lip was quivering. Then her face hardened, and when she spoke again a hint of anger laced her words. "Did you forget that I'm the one who tried to get Neptune for us? Not you!"

Shannon stepped back, silent for a moment, and Ashley continued, her voice softening. "We could get a foal tomorrow. We really could!" she finished.

Mom put an arm around Shannon and pulled her close. The cotton candy smashed into the side of Mom's purse, but she didn't seem to notice or care. "I know how you're feeling," Mom said gently. "But you can't blame your sister. She really did try to get that foal." Mom grinned at Ashley and then turned back to Shannon. "Your dad and I warned you that you might not get a foal this year." She pushed Shannon's light brown bangs from her forehead. "You might have to work another summer and save more money. Just keep saving. "Someday you'll get your pony."

Taking a deep breath, Shannon wiped a stray tear from her cheek.

"What you give in life is exactly what you get back," Mom said. "You have given a lot to others, and one of these days you will get all the things you dream of in return."

Shannon leaned into Mom's shoulder. She thought of all the hours she had volunteered for the Therapeutic Riding Program, and all the times she and her sister had gone with their 4-H club to nursing homes to share animals with older folks. At that moment she decided she believed her Mom. She forced a smile and then turned to Ashley. "I'm sorry." she said. "It's not your fault."

Ashley's face brightened. "It's okay. I think I know how you feel." She took Shannon's hand and squeezed it tight. "Let's go back and look at the ponies again," she suggested. "I heard someone say the firemen have tagged them. We can write down the numbers of our favorite ones, so we're ready to bid tomorrow."

Most of the foals in the pens now wore yellow paper tags on their rumps, glued tight. Each tag bore a number for the auction. The pony foals without tags were the ones the firemen wanted to keep for their own herds. Still, buyers would purchase them and donate back to the island. Shannon knew they got a picture of the foal, and a certificate saying their foal would live on Assateague Island for all of its life. Buying a turn-back foal would be nice, but that is not what she dreamed of. As she looked at the foals, Shannon couldn't help but hope again.

Mom pulled a small spiral notebook from her purse and handed it to Shannon along with a pen. "It wouldn't hurt to write down the numbers of the ones you like best," she said, echoing Ashley's words.

"Look at that one," Ashley said, pointing to a tiny chestnut foal with one white sock.

"It's cute," Shannon said, "but it's too small. We want something out of the taller herds so we won't outgrow it too soon."

"That's good solid thinking," Dad agreed. "Some of the bigger herds have had Mustang horses bred into them."

Ashley's eyebrows rose in two question marks over her dark eyes. "What's that mean?"

"It means that Mustang horses from out West were brought to the island and added to the herds years ago, probably to make the ponies grow larger. The herds with Mustang in them are bigger now." Dad smiled. "An Arabian stallion named Premiere also made the herds grow larger than those on the Maryland side of Assateague Island."

"Like that one over there," Shannon added, pointing to a chestnut stallion standing over a bunch of mares of mixed colors and several foals. He was big.

"Yes, like that one," Dad said. "Look at some of his babies!"

Shannon's eyes lit up as she looked. Many of his foals were bays, tall and leggy. Some had white socks and blazes, and others were solid colored. There were a few pintos and a chestnut colored one, too. Shannon recognized the foal she had touched by the fence, earlier. She opened the notebook and began to write down numbers, starting with his: Number 49.

"Ooh, Shannon, look there!"

Following her sister, Shannon saw a big buckskin stallion and a brown pinto mare. Beside them was a very small chestnut pinto, the tiniest of any of the foals she had seen yet. He was bony and angular with the look of a newborn.

"That foal was born just last night," a man standing next to them said. "The mother was one of the mares that were brought over earlier in the week, on the trailer."

Shannon grinned at the tiny foal. He would be sold in the auction as a fall pick-up, one the buyer would have to come back for in the fall.

"Do you have all the numbers you need?" Dad asked.

"We could never write down all the good ones," Ashley answered. "There are too many to find them all!"

"I think you have enough," Mom said. "You'll change your mind tomorrow anyway, when they come out in the auction ring.

"Tomorrow!" Ashley squealed. "Just one more day!"

That night it took Shannon a long time to get to sleep. On the walls of the tent she watched the shadows of other campers at their campfires. She breathed deep, inhaling the smell of a musty tent and listened to the muffled sounds of conversation and occasional laughter. She watched the green digits on the travel alarm clock turn over, minute by minute. Finally she slept fitfully, dreaming of ponies running wild. She awoke, and then slept again, foals prancing through the thread of her dreams. She was awake before first light, watching the numbers turn over on the clock and wishing the alarm would sound so their big day could begin.

Chapter Eight

By 6:40 in the morning, the back of the carnival grounds was milling with people. Firemen had set up an area for the pony auction, one that included a shaded pavilion where the auctioneer would stand. A large grassy area had been fenced off in front. This gave the firemen a place to show off the foals to prospective buyers.

Already, lawn chairs lined the front and one side of the makeshift ring. Shannon and her family felt lucky to get the last front row spaces on one side. Mom and Dad set up their lawn chairs, and Shannon and Ashley settled cross-legged on a blanket beside them. Ashley had found a sea gull feather and put it in her hair, behind her ear. By 7:15 a.m. the lawn chairs were at least eight rows deep.

A fireman adjusting the ropes in front of the girls stopped to smile at them. "Are you going to buy a colt today?" he asked.

"We hope so," Shannon answered.

"We will," Ashley chimed in. "We've been coming here every year since we were little, and now we have five hundred and forty-eight dollars saved to buy one!"

"Five hundred and forty-eight dollars, huh?" the fireman mused.

Shannon felt the knot of worry in her stomach. "Do you think we'll get one for that price?"

The fireman took off his cap, scratched his head, and then replaced the cap.

Shannon read his tag, Chincoteague Fireman, David Savage.

"Hard to tell," Mr. Savage said slowly. "Sometimes you can get one that low. But they've been selling for a lot more the past few years." He turned

to go and then stopped. "I'll tell you what, if you get close, I'll throw in $25 to help you along."

Ashley's eyes got big. "Really?"

"Sure!" He tapped Ashley on the arm as he passed. "Remember, twenty-five dollars extra from me if you need it."

Shannon smiled at his back when the fireman strolled away, checking the ropes as he went.

The first foal came out at exactly 8 a.m. It was a chestnut filly, small in stature, with a white star on her forehead and one white stocking.

"Who'll start the bidding at a thousand?" the auctioneer asked.

Shannon sucked in her breath. A thousand dollars for the first foal?

When no one responded the auctioneer lowered the amount to five hundred, then three hundred. Finally, the bidding began at two hundred dollars. Shannon relaxed a little. The auctioneer's voice hummed, like a bow being pulled across the strings of a violin. As his sing-song voice rose and fell the bids went up and up, until the filly was sold for six hundred and fifty dollars.

Shannon let out the breath she hadn't realized she was holding.

"Shannon," Ashley said softly. "If that little one went for six hundred and fifty dollars, I think we're in trouble. We'll never get a big one for five hundred and forty-eight dollars!"

Shannon reached over and touched Ashley's knee. "Sometimes the first one goes for a high price, no matter what it looks like," she said. But, inside, her stomach did a flip-flop, the knot tightening. She was worried, too.

As each foal came out the price went higher and higher, with the third foal selling for over a thousand dollars. Shannon twirled her hair nervously. "Maybe we should bid," she said, "just to let them know we are here."

"Good idea," Mom said. "Why don't you go ahead and bid on the next one. But don't go over five hundred and fifty dollars!"

"You want us to do the bidding?"

Dad smiled and nodded at Shannon. "It will be your foal, not ours. Now, go ahead. Just raise your hand and call out a bid."

Shannon wrung her hands. "You do it," she told Ashley. "I can't!"

"Okay!" Ashley seemed excited, happy to have something to do. "Which one should I bid on?"

"Bid on all of them," Shannon answered without hesitation. "At these prices we can't be picky."

Ashley nodded solemnly, the white feather bobbing in her hair.

A moment later a foal was led out. He was a bay and white pinto colt who reared into the air. The two firemen holding him quickly brought him down.

The colt's eyes rolled and he pawed the ground and then sidestepped, almost getting away.

"Well, he sure is a spunky one," the auctioneer said. "What do I hear for this little guy?"

"Five hundred dollars!" Ashley shouted. She waved both hands at the auctioneer and her voice was so loud Shannon jumped.

"Hey, folks, this little girl has a five hundred dollar bid! Now, how about that? We'll start him at five hundred. Do I hear six hundred?"

As quickly as she had shouted, Ashley's bid was left behind in a sea of rising bids: six hundred, seven hundred, seven-fifty, nine hundred... The auctioneer's voice hummed, until the colt sold for twelve hundred dollars.

Shannon leaned over Ashley. "Don't worry," she said. "You were good. But next time start the bidding lower."

Ashley bid two hundred dollars on the next foal, but the bids quickly soared over five hundred dollars. She tried to get a bid in on the next foal, and the next, but the price quickly rose above five hundred on each.

"You bid," she told Shannon, her eyes downcast. "Maybe you'll be lucky." So Shannon began bidding on foals, first a bay pinto, then a black one with tall white stockings and a tiny star on its forehead. It wasn't long before they were taking turns bidding. But even the tiniest, muddiest, wildest, and ugliest foals went for more money than Shannon and Ashley had saved.

A boy about their age, wearing a pair of bib overalls, jumped into the air and let out a whoop when his parents were the final bid on a buckskin foal that went for twelve hundred dollars. Tears filled Shannon's eyes. Last year she would have smiled at his success, but this year it only made her sad.

An hour and 39 foals later, they hadn't even come close. Shannon knew they only had 53 foals to sell this year. Each year the number was different, depending on how many were born during the year. There was only enough food and space for the fire department to keep about one hundred fifty ponies on Assateague.

The knot in Shannon's stomach had become almost unbearable. She wouldn't get a foal. She knew that now and as the realization sank in she felt sick. She thought about all her summer work, all her saving. Her hopes had been for nothing. Another summer vacation at Chincoteague Island had been spent wishing. Even though this time they had money, they would go home without a foal again.

She watched as the next foal was led out. Beside her, Ashley's eyes were down, her hands still in her lap. "I'm not going to bid," she said. "Why should I?"

"Me, too," Shannon said sadly, giving up. She felt Mom rub her shoulder gently, and watched as Dad pulled Ashley into his lap.

"Here, Shannon," Ashley said, plucking one white feather from her hair. "You hold one for luck."

Shannon tried to smile at Ashley, but she wasn't sure the smile made it all the way out. She twirled the feather between her fingers and watched the next foal come out. It was another big bay, but this one had long white stockings that reached halfway up his legs, and a tiny white spot on his forehead.

Shannon blurred her eyes on purpose, looking past him. He was perfect, and she didn't want to see. Instead, she looked at the fireman they had spoken to earlier. What was his name? David Savage, she remembered. He was talking to a pretty lady wearing a floppy straw hat. Beside her was a tall man with dark hair and a broad smile.

The foal moved closer until the firemen held him in place almost directly in front of Shannon. She stole a glance, and her breath stuck in her throat. It was number 49. She'd watched him in the pens. He was perfect! His brown eyes rolled wildly. Then he stopped, and standing still his eyes met hers. She felt as though the bay foal was looking into her soul, as though he was her very own.

Tears filled Shannon's eyes. She forced herself to look away. Rubbing her face, she looked across the ring again. The fireman, Mr. Savage, was pointing right at her! No. He couldn't be pointing at her. He must be pointing at the foal, she thought, but the three of them began walking toward them.

"This is Carollynn and Ed," Mr. Savage said a moment later. "They want to help your children buy a pony."

Mom smiled, but Dad shook his head. "That's okay," he said. "Thanks anyway."

The woman was smiling and she put her hand on Shannon's shoulder. Behind them the bidding on the bay foal was rising. Someone had bid $600.

"I came to the island to buy a foal for a child," Miss Carollynn said.

Dad looked bewildered. "There are lots of kids here who want a pony," he said. "Mine can save another year."

Why is he saying that? Shannon wondered.

But the lady did not give up. She took her hat off. Her hair was thin underneath, just growing in again from being shaved. "I had a tumor removed," she said, "and I made it through the surgery, cancer-free. If you get a gift in life, you have to give it back."

Mom brushed at her cheek. Was she crying?

"I came to buy a foal for a child, to give back for the gift of life I received."

There was silence, and then she surged on. "It is supposed to be your girls'," she declared. "Everywhere I went when I was sick I found feathers. I thought God was sending me a message that I would be okay. And now, I see your daughter has a feather in her ponytail and your other daughter has one in her hand. I think I am supposed to help them get their pony."

Ashley and her lucky feathers!

"Let me help them get their pony!"

The crowd around us began to mumble, and then to chant, "Let her buy it!"

Shannon's heart pounded harder than ocean surf when Dad nodded.

Behind us the bay foal was rounding the ring again. "Do I hear $1,000?" the auctioneer asked.

"One thousand," the lady yelled.

The leggy foal pranced out from under the firemen who held him tightly around the neck, pulling them across the ring for a moment or two until they gained control. Oh, he was so perfect!

Then Shannon heard the auctioneer yell, "Sold, for a thousand dollars," and for a moment she didn't know who had bought the perfect colt. Then she saw the auctioneer point their way and she knew. The perfect bay colt was going home with them.

Chapter Nine

"God took care of me in my time of greatest need," Miss Carollynn said, and they all hugged. For the first time, Shannon realized that the woman held a tiny white feather in her hand. She sucked in her breath. Something as simple as her breathing could interfere with the story. There should be no sound, only Miss Carollynn's lilting voice.

"I meant it when I said I found feathers everywhere, even in the oddest places," she explained. "Then, once day, I found Psalm 91, verse four in the Bible. The verse said the Lord would cover me with feathers and protect me. I knew those feathers were a sign sent to give me faith."

Shannon's mind was spinning. She couldn't stop thinking about her new foal, her own miracle. At the same time she was caught up in Miss Carollynn's story. She handed her feather to the woman and Miss Carollynn took it gently.

"I collect them, you know." She smiled broadly.

Tears came all at once. They rolled down Shannon's cheeks and she didn't try to stop them. She was thinking about Miss Carollynn's story, the part about giving something back. Mom has always taught us that, she thought, and what Miss Carollynn is saying is the same thing. You get what you give in life. And sometimes you have to give it back, too.

"Let's go see your new colt!" Miss Carollynn took her hand.

The perfect colt, Shannon thought. The tall bay.

As they walked to the booth to pay for the foal Shannon realized they still had raffle tickets for the ladies auxiliary pony which wouldn't be drawn until the next day. If we win it, she thought, we'll pass it on, just like Miss Carollynn and Mr. Ed. We'll help another child's dream come true.

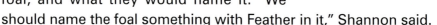

As they walked she thought about their foal, and what they would name it. "We should name the foal something with Feather in it," Shannon said.

"Ocean Feather," Ashley said dreamily. She was skipping along beside them, her hand in Miss Carollynn's other hand.

"Or Sea Feather," Shannon said.

"Yes!" Ashley shouted. Then she giggled, a ripple of joy that caught Shannon off guard.

"Sea Feather!" Mom repeated.

"It's perfect," Miss Carollynn said. She put her hand across Shannon's shoulder. Shannon looked at Dad and saw he was smiling down at her.

They approached the pen and leaned against the fence. All of them were looking for the foal with number forty-nine on his rump. Then Shannon saw him. "There!"

Everyone looked to see. The foal turned slowly to meet them and Shannon saw a splash of white.

Miss Carollynn and Mom gasped.

"He has a feather on his neck!" Mr. Ed said in disbelief.

It was true! The foal was not a solid bay, but a bay pinto, for there on his neck Shannon could clearly see a white marking. It was not a perfectly shaped feather, but definitely a feather! Except for his four white stockings, the jagged feather shape was the only display of white on the pony's body.

"Sea Feather," she whispered as the foal moved closer. Without taking her eyes off the foal, she reached over to grab Ashley's hand. "We have our foal," she whispered. "Our very own foal!"

Glossary

Island Terms:

Assateague Island - Assateague Island is a thirty-three mile long island which lies along the coast of Maryland and Virginia. Wild ponies inhabit the island. On the Virginia side, (the side that borders Chincoteague Island) Assateague is a wildlife refuge.

Chincoteague Island - An island off the coast of Virginia on the East Coast of the United States. The island is seven miles long and one and a half miles wide and is known for its harvest of seafood, and the wild pony swim and auction which is held during the last week of July each year. Chincoteague was named by an early Indian Tribe, and it means beautiful land across the waters. Chincoteague Island is one of the few islands in the world that is actually below sea level. If not for the barrier island of Assateague, Chincoteague Island would be washed away by the ocean!

Chincoteague Ponies - The Assateague Island ponies that live on the Virginia half of Assateague, are fenced off from the ones on the Maryland side, and they are called The Chincoteague Ponies. The Chincoteague Volunteer Fire Company owns the Chincoteague Ponies and they have made concentrated effort to improve the breed by introducing several other breeds into the herds, including Mustangs. The resulting pony herds are just as hardy, but more refined. The Chincoteague Ponies now have a registry.

Pony Penning -   Each year the Chincoteague Volunteer Fire Department rounds up all the ponies on the Virginia side of Assateague Island. These saltwater cowboys herd the ponies into the narrowest part of the bay at slack tide, and swim them to Chincoteague Island, bringing them ashore at Memorial Park. After a brief rest, the ponies are paraded from Memorial Park to the Chincoteague Fire Department's carnival grounds. They always swim the last Wednesday of July. They are always auctioned off on the last Thursday of July, and returned to the island of Assateague on Friday. This tradition began over 300 years ago as way of controlling herd size, but it became much more. Over the years it has become a fundraiser for the fire department, and a time of great fun and celebration. Pony Penning was made famous in 1947 when Marguerite Henry's famous children's book, *Misty of Chincoteague* was published.

Sika Deer - Originally brought to the east coast by Boy Scouts, the Oriental elk called the Sika deer are a common site on Assateague Island. They are much smaller than the whitetail deer that are native to the area. Over 800 Sika Deer live on Chincoteague Island. They can often be seen grazing by the sides of the roads and trails.

Whitetail Deer - Whitetail deer are native to the east coast. The Chincoteague Island Refuge is home to about 200 whitetail deer. They are more shy than the Sika deer that live on the refuge.

Equine Terms:

Colt - A boy foal.

Filly - A girl foal.

Foal - A baby horse or pony.

Forelock - The long hair that grows between the ears of a horse or pony and falls across their forehead.

Mane - The long hair that grows from the neck of a horse or pony from behind the ears to   the start of the back.

Mare - A mature female horse or pony.

Pony - A horse that is under 14.2 hands in height. Horses are measured from the highest point of the withers (high point of the back) to the ground. Each hand equals 4 inches.

Stallion - A mature male horse or pony that is still able to father young.

Tack - Equipment specifically for horses. Some most used tack includes, saddles, bridles, halters, saddle pads, and other more specific equipment.

Tail - The long hair that grows from the back of a horse in the same way a puppy or a cat has a tail.

Yearling - A horse or pony that is one year old.

Chincoteague Pony Colors:

Bay - A dark brown horse or pony with a black mane and tail, nose, muzzle and legs. The black is known as black tips. A bay horse may or may not have white legs, or a white marking on the face.

Black - Solid black with a black mane and tail.

Buckskin - A golden or palomino-colored horse with a black nose, ear tips, and black coloring on the legs. A buckskin may or may not have white legs or a white marking on the face.

Chestnut - A reddish brown horse or pony with a flaxen, cream colored, or reddish colored mane and tail. Chestnut colored horses are often described as being the color of a new copper penny.

Palomino - A golden colored horse with a cream or flaxen mane and tail.

Pinto - A pinto horse can be white with splotches of color (such as chestnut, bay, palomino or black) or one of those colors with large spots of white. Chincoteague is known for their many flashy pinto ponies.

Roan – A solid colored horse whose coloring is sprinkled with white hairs.

Sorrel – A light chestnut